Adolph C. Lent, James Swords, Thomas Swords

## An Inaugural Dissertation

shewing in what manner pestilential vapours acquire their acid quality,

and how this is neutralized and destroyed by alkalies

Adolph C. Lent, James Swords, Thomas Swords

**An Inaugural Dissertation**
*shewing in what manner pestilential vapours acquire their acid quality, and how this is neutralized and destroyed by alkalies*

ISBN/EAN: 9783337382858

Printed in Europe, USA, Canada, Australia, Japan

Cover: Foto ©Andreas Hilbeck / pixelio.de

More available books at **www.hansebooks.com**

AN

# INAUGURAL DISSERTATION,

SHEWING IN WHAT MANNER

## PESTILENTIAL VAPOURS

Acquire their *acid* Quality, and how this is neutralized and deftroyed by

## *ALKALIES.*

SUBMITTED TO THE PUBLIC EXAMINATION OF THE
FACULTY OF PHYSIC, UNDER THE AUTHORITY
OF THE TRUSTEES OF COLUMBIA COLLEGE,
IN THE STATE OF NEW-YORK,

WILLIAM SAMUEL JOHNSON, LL. D. President.

FOR THE DEGREE OF

## DOCTOR OF PHYSIC,

*On the 2d Day of May,* 1798.

———

*By* ADOLPH C. LENT,

Citizen of the State of New-York.

CNOMES! to impede the DEMON's deadly courfe,
YOUR BANDS CELESTIAL marfhall'd all their force:
From watery caves where fhelly nations fleep,
From finuous bays, from Ocean's briny deep,
YOUR hands collecting fpread thro' every clime,
A fair proportion of attempering LIME;
Thro' all the fpace terreftrial Nature owns,
Of Climates, Colures, Longitudes and Zones,
YOUR fearch the powerful ALKALIS has found,
And caft, the Earth's circumference around,
The friendly powers of METAL, OIL and CLAY,
With duteous zeal your juft commands obey;
With wife difpatch their various ftations gain,
And guard the Mine, the Mountain, and the Plain.
MITCHILL.

NEW-YORK:

Printed by T. & J. SWORDS, Printers to the Faculty of Phyfic of
Columbia College, No. 99 Pearl-ftreet.
—1798.—

# INTRODUCTION.

*General Ideas of the Diſorganization of Bodies after Death.*

$A$LL animal and vegetable bodies, deprived of the principle of life, undergo certain changes, by which their texture becomes deſtroyed, and their compoſition altered; having loſt the chemical affinity ſubſiſting between their elementary principles in their living ſtate. The proceſs by which this decompoſition is effected, which renders more ſimple the compounds formed by vegetation and animalization, and cauſes them to enter into new combinations of different kinds, is named putrefaction, and is determined by the ſame cauſes, agents, and circumſtances, in both, viz. oxygenous air, caloric, and water. Upon a proper application of theſe agents does the more rapid or ſlow diſſolution of theſe bodies depend. Animal ſubſtances, compoſed of hydrogene, carbone, oxygene, and ſepton (azote), and not unfrequently ſtill more complex by the addition of ſulphur, phoſphorus, iron, lime, and ſoda, when deprived of that conſtitution which imparts to them life, and expoſed to the influence of theſe agents, are ſoon altered by more ſimple attractions between their elements, which moſt generally have a tendency to unite in binary

or ternary combinations. This new affociation between their principles gives rife to new bodies, fuch
as feptous (azotic) air, oxyd of fepton (azote),
feptous acid, feptic gas, feptic acid, feptic acid gas,
carbonic acid gas, hydrogenous gas, oxygenous gas,
carbonated, fulphurated, and phofphorated hydrogenous gas, foda, water, and perhaps ammonia,
which gradually efcape into the atmofphere, proportionally diminifhing the putrifying mafs. Upon
the union of thefe elements all the changes refult-
ing from the putrefaction of animal bodies depend.
In the union of fepton (azote) and oxygene, *according as the acidifying principle unites with fepton in a
greater or lefs quantity*, we perceive the formation
of feptous gas, and the oxyd of fepton, feptous
and feptic acid, and feptic acid gas; to the production of which it is well known how much animal fubftances contribute; as in nitre-beds, graves,
ditches, puddles, &c. and in all thofe places where
putrefaction takes place to any large amount. The
combination of carbon and oxygene with caloric,
explains the generation of carbonic acid gas. The
carbon and hydrogene may unite in the form of fat,
or that fubftance fo often defcribed as refembling
fpermacæti; and if ammonia is formed, it will proceed from the union of fepton with hydrogene. It
is poffible, alfo, in bodies containing fulphur and
phofphorus, thefe acidifiable bafes may unite with
oxygene, and form their refpective acids. Where
lime (calcareous earth), foda, or iron, is extricated
by putrefaction, thefe bafes may attach the carbonic,
feptic, fulphuric, and phofphoric acids, and form

carbonates, feptites, fulphats, and phofphates of lime, foda, and iron. Thefe are the products, liable, however, to variation, which are evolved on the putrefaction of animal fubftances. It may happen that all, or a greater part of the fepton, may combine with caloric, and fly off in this ftate in the form of feptous gas: on the contrary, all the fepton may unite with oxygene, and be converted into feptic acid. The fame variations may take place in the other combinations, according as the elementary principles get within the fpheres of each other's attraction, and according to the varying proportions of the agents above enumerated.

The products which obtain, on the decompofition of vegetables, are nearly the fame with thofe of animals; except that the compounds, into which fepton, fulphur, and phofphorus enter, are not fo often formed; nor are the feptic compounds produced in fo great plenty, owing to a lefs quantity of fepton in the latter than in the former fubftances;—the greater part of vegetables containing little or none, though others are furnifhed plentifully with it. Vegetable fubftances, though liable to undergo diforganization, are not fo much fo as animal; their order of compofition being lefs complex: neither do they afford fo much feptous gas when acted upon by the feptic acid, nor contribute in fo eminent a degree to the formation of this acid. Thefe different appearances between the two fubftances, and the more rapid decay of animal bodies, feem to depend on the prefence of one elementary principle only, namely, fepton, being in a greater abundance in animal than in vegetable fubftances. It appears probable, therefore, that by the addition of this principle to vegetable matter, it may be made to poffefs fimilar qualities with that of animal; and by depriving the latter of its fepton, it will become, in fome meafure, vegetable. This may be termed the capital difference between the two fubftances: but other phenomena, whofe influence on the animal compofition is, no doubt, inferior, ought likewife to be noticed; fuch as the phofphoric acid, and its combinations with lime, ammonia, and foda; the quality of the refidue of animal matter, after diffolution, being principally owing to thefe combinations.*

---

* Vide Fourcroi's Philof. of Chemiftry, p. 162, 163.

# CHAPTER I.

*Relations of the Products of Animal and Vegetable Decompofition to other Bodies.*

ANIMAL and vegetable matter having been fhewn, on diffolution, to give rife to new compounds, fuch as the feptic oxyds and acids, &c and as all living fyftems, whether of plants or animals, muft lofe the principle by which their life is continued, and become diforganized, the quantities of thofe gafeous fluids which are naturally formed and diffufed through the air in fuch proceffes, muft be immenfe, and exceed ordinary eftimation. From the perpetual accumulation of thefe gafeous bodies, it would feem the refpirability of the atmofphere muft, within a fhort period, become deftroyed, and, from the noxious and even poifonous qualities of certain of thefe gafes, fuch as the feptic compounds, acquire a deleterious and deftructive operation on the conftitution of man, and other animals who live and move in it. This, from appearances, would really happen, were it not that thefe gafeous fubftances did again enter into union with certain other bodies, on coming within the fpheres of their attractions, by which they are taken out of circulation, and become fixed or decompounded.

1. In this manner the oxyd and acid of fepton, on meeting with certain bodies, are taken out of circulation, and become fixed or neutralized, and thus reftrained from exercifing their deleterious

qualities, which, if left to pervade the atmofphere, would, on meeting the bodies of men, carry on their deftructive and corroding operation, and produce difeafes of different grades and malignancy, in proportion as the attendant circumftances, and the conftitution of each, were more or lefs favourable to their operation.—The principal of thofe bodies which have the power to coerce and reftrain this acid, is pot-afh, or the vegetable alkali, alfo called falt of wormwood, and falt of tartar, with which the acid unites, and forms the feptite of pot-afh, commonly known by the name of falt-petre, or nitre, from which this acid has derived the name hitherto moft commonly affixed to it. This faline fubftance, afforded by the combuftion of plants, has the ftrongeft attraction of all bodies prefent, where putrefaction takes place, for the feptic acid,* and will, confequently, difengage the acid from all other bodies with which it is united, and attract it itfelf.—There are certain foils and tracts of country, as in Spain, Perfia, and the Eaft-Indies, where pot-afh is native, and by abforbing from putrid and all other bodies with which they meet, all the acid they contain, they change to feptite of pot-afh (nitre). Where this fubftance is not naturally prefent, it is frequently accumulated from adventitious circumftances; near the habitations of men it is generally produced by the agency of fire; and large quantities of it, diffolved in water, are continually thrown away with fuch folutions as have

* Vide Bergman's Tab. of Elec. Attrac,

been employed to aid common water in cleanfing, and anfwering the purpofes of wafhing.\* In fuch inftances, where there is no pot-afh prefent, or there is more of the acid than it is capable to neutralize, it may be arrefted by the muriate of foda (common or culinary falt), which is confumed in large quantities by men and brute animals. The alkaline bafis of the falt having a ftronger attraction for the feptic than muriatic acid, it will diffolve its connection with the latter, and form a union with the former, in the form of feptite of foda (cubic or quadrangular nitre). This acid likewife unites readily with calcareous earth (lime), converting it into a feptite of lime (calcareous nitre). From the greater abundance in which lime is found in and about human dwellings, old walls, finks, drains, &c. than either of the above alkalies, it might be prefumed, that this acid, in conjunction with calcareous earth, would very commonly obtain. This is found to happen. The nitrous quality of old walls, plaiftered with lime, which takes place even to fuch an extent, as to have become worthy the attention of perfons engaged in the manufacturing of nitre, is fufficient evidence of the ftrong affinity which fubfifts between it and the acid; at the fame time proving this acid to be prefent within and around human dwellings, in confiderable quantity. Clay likewife has an affinity

---

\* See a calculation, made by Profeffor MITCHILL, of the immenfe quantity of this alkali diffolved in water, which is, from time to time, thrown out in large and populous cities, in New-York Mag. for January, 1797, p. 9.

for this acid; and in such walls where lime is one of the ingredients, and becomes faturated with the feptic acid, the clay will unite with it, and be converted into an argillaceous feptite (aluminous nitre). Its affinity, however, is in fo weak a degree, that where either of the alkalies, or lime, is prefent, its union with the acid will be prevented, or diffolved, if made. This acid alfo unites with the volatile alkali, for which, next to the fixed alkalies and lime, it has the greateft attraction; but from the rare occurrence of this alkali in the earth, it will rarely happen that a feptite of ammonia is formed. Fat, or oily fubftances, will likewife unite with this acid, and that with fuch rapidity as to burft into flame with many kinds of oils. " The action of the nitric (feptic) acid on moft inflammable matters, confifts in nothing more than a continual decompofition of this acid."—" The nitric (feptic) acid, when mixed with oils, renders them thick and black, converts them into charcoal, or inflames them, according as the acid is more or lefs concentrated, or in greater or lefs quantity."* From the experiments of Margraff and other chemifts, this acid was alfo found in rain and fnow waters; and from the difpofition of water to enter into union with it, may it be learned how rain-water in fhowers acquires the unwholefome qualities which, in certain inftances, it has been obferved to exert on the conftitution.

Hence, then, it appears, that the alkalies, calca-

* Fourcroi, &c. Chaptal's Chemiftry, p. 133, &c.

reous earths, clay, oils, and water, on meeting the feptic acid, act in a beneficial manner, by repreffing and keeping down this fluid, which, by rifing in the atmofphere, and pervading human dwellings, &c. might occafion intermittent, or other fevers of a more malignant or peftilential nature.

2. Carbonic acid (fixed air), which is fo plentifully formed during the putrefactive procefs from animal and vegetable bodies, by reafon of its greater fpecific gravity, never rifes to any great height in the air, but defcends to the furface of the earth, where it may either be abforbed by lime, or may contribute to the nourifhment of plants, which poffefs the power of decompounding and abforbing it, when in a fmall quantity.*

3 and 4. The hydrogene, or inflammable gas, that is fometimes extricated during putrefaction, efcapes, and mingles in the air with other gafes, with fome of which, more efpecially the oxygenous it may unite, and form water; while the oxygene gas that is fet loofe in certain inftances, may afcend and replenifh, in part, the perpetual wafte which this fluid, from combuftion, refpiration, &c. muft neceffarily fuffer, from time to time, in the atmofphere.

5. The other gafeous compounds, to which the difagreeable fmell and phofphorefcent appearance attending vegetable and animal putrefaction are principally owing, may combine with certain bodies they meet with, or afcend in the atmofphere, from whence they may again be precipitated to the earth.

* Chapt. Chem. vol. iii. p. 32.

## CHAPTER II.

*Facts tending to shew the Connection between the Ef-*
*fluvia of putrefying Bodies, and malignant and pes-*
*tilential Diseases.*

FROM marsh exhalations and human effluvia,
has it been believed, from the earliest ages of phyfic to the present time, that malignant and pestilential difeafes derived their origin. Daily experience
still confirms that it is in the neighbourhood of
marshes, and all such places where vegetable and
animal putrefaction takes place to any extent, that
pestilential and other difeafes of various grades and
violence prevail. Epidemics, attended with car-
buncles and buboes, which are denominated, in conjunction with the ordinary symptoms of what is called
*jail* and *hospital* fever, the characteristics of the
plague, down to the mildest intermittent, have appeared, and raged with extreme violence, occasioned
by the exhalations from putrefying animal and vegetable substances.* .

The numerous facts and observations of the most
judicious writers shew, that there are few climates
where instances have not occurred of malignant
epidemic and endemic difeafes, occasioned by an
atmosphere surcharged and poisoned with the effluvia exhaled from certain putrid vegetable and
animal substances. Bengal, on both sides the river
Ganges, and Egypt, annually overflowed by the

---

* Pringle on the Army, p. 321 and 322.

Nile, experience an unhealthy and pestilential atmosphere, immediately after the exhalations from
the putrefying collections of vegetable and animal
matter begin to arise in the air, and bring on diseases
of various grades of malignancy, down to what is
called the plague. The same occurs in every cli-
mate in a greater or less extent. In ponds, ditches,
swamps, &c. where, after the evaporation of the
water, the collections of vegetable and animal matter being left bare, and exposed to the influence of
the sun, begin to putrefy, and emit certain gaseous
exhalations, which transfuse themselves into the atmosphere, and produce diseases of an intermittent
or more malignant type, proportionate to the concentrated state of the contagion, and other conco-
mitant circumstances. Lind, whose testimony,
from his experience, must equal most authors, re-
lates abundance of instances where what is called
*yellow fever*, and other malignant diseases, were
caused by gaseous fluids, exhaled from low and
marshy places, exposed to the influence of a powerful sun. He observes, that " in all spots, in the
East-Indies, situated near large swamps, or the mud-
dy banks of rivers, or the foul shores of the sea, the
vapours exhaling from putrid stagnated water, from
the corrupted vegetable, and other impurities, produce mortal diseases."* The same author more
particularly mentions, that the *yellow fever* often
raged at Greenwich Hospital, in Jamaica, which,
he observes, was built near a marsh, and could not

* Lind on Hot Climates, p. 85.

proceed from any fource of infection in the hofpital. He every where attributes the *yellow fever* to the vapours arifing from putrefying vegetable and animal fubftances.

Dr. Clark, in his Obfervations on the Difeafes of long Voyages to hot Countries,* mentions a *contagious malignant* fever, which prevailed at Prince's Ifland, in 1771, produced from the exhalations of putrefying vegetable fubftances.

The plague which caufed fo great a terror and mortality in London, in 1625 and 1636, according to the account given by Mr. Woodal, furgeon to St. Bartholomew's Hofpital, and furgeon-general to the Eaft-India Company, who was prefent thofe two years during its prevalence, was evidently generated in that city, from the gafeous exhalations of putrid collections of animal and vegetable matter. He fays, " the terreftrial caufes (after mentioning it as a punifhment inflicted on mankind for their fins,) are, by common confent of moft writers, as followeth; venomous and ftinking vapours, arifing from ftanding ponds, or pooles, ditches, lakes, dunghills, finks, channels, vaults, or the like; as alfo unclean flaughter-houfes of beafts, dead carcafes of men, as in time of war, and of ftinking fifh, fowl, or any thing that hath contained life and is putrid: as alfo, more particularly in great cities, as in London, the unclean keeping of houfes, lanes, alleys, and ftreets: from thofe recited, and the like infectious venomous vapours, by warmth of the

* Vol. i. p. 123 and 124.

fun exhaled, are apt and able to infect the living bodies of men, and thereby to produce the plague,
as experience too much sheweth."* From the de-
scription given by Mead† of Grand-Cairo, the sup-
posed harbinger of a species of the worst type of dis-
ease, the plague, it will appear to be produced by
similar causes with the above case, viz. by certain
gases formed on the putrefaction of vegetable and
animal substances, and suffered to arise into and
poison the circumambient atmosphere with their
noxious and stimulating qualities. He says, " it
is situated in a sandy plain, at a foot of a mountain,
which, by keeping off the winds that would refresh
the air, makes the heat very stifling. Through the
midst of it passes a canal, which is filled with water
during the overflowing of the Nile, and, after the
river is decreased, it gradually dries up. Into this
canal the people throw all kinds of filth, carrion, &c.
so that the stench arising from it, and the mud together, is insufferable. In this situation of things,
the plague every year constantly preys upon the inhabitants, and is only stopt when the Nile, by overflowing, washes away the load of filth."

Pringle, Jackson, Hume, and a number of other
authors, might be added in further proof, that the
effluvia from animal and vegetable putrefaction
may give rise to, and are the common causes of malignant and pestilential diseases. Instances, abun-
dantly numerous, occur in our own territory, to
confirm the noxious and pestilential influence of

* Monro on the Army, vol. i. note to p. 223.
† On the Plague, p. 29 and 30.

the products juft named, on their application to the conftitution, notwithftanding the (fo named) *facts*, which were promifed *fpeedily to appear* almoft a year fince, in contradiction of this opinion. It is related by Dr. Reynolds,* that from the putrefaction of a horfe, which lay on the borders of a marfhy piece of ground; a young woman who lived near, and was obliged frequently to pafs and repafs the putrid car- cafe, was affected with violent pains in the head, and ficknefs at her ftomach. On the fecond day of attack was bled, but her fever increafed, and fhe became delirious. A number of blifters, furround- ed by inflammation, appeared upon her feet and hands, fingers and toes; and fhe died the fourth day.

A cafe, a few years fince, occurred in this city, where a fevere attack of fever, of the remittent type, attended with petechiæ, made its appearance in two perfons of the fame family. On examination into the caufe of thefe complaints, it was difcovered, by the attending phyfician, to have originated from the blood and other offal of cattle, flaughtered in the yard belonging to the houfe, which was fuffered to collect and putrefy, to the exhalations of which the two perfons attacked had been, from time to time, expofed. An inftance of a fimilar nature, which occurred to a practitioner of a neighbouring town, is related by Mr. Bayley, in his treatife on the epi- demic of New-York in 1795.† " Some time in the month of September I was called to vifit a young man about eighteen years old, in a family in

* Webfter's Collection, p. 197.
† P. 84 & feq.

the fkirt of the (Hartford) town. He was violently
attacked with moft of the characteriftic fymptoms
of yellow fever, &c. The next day a fecond was
taken in the fame manner; and, on the morning of
the third, three more were taken fick. This led
me to fufpect fome particular caufe. I fearched
for it in vain that time. The next morning, on
paffing through the kitchen, I fmelt fomething that
was very offenfive, which none of the family had noticed. On opening the cellar-door, I found that it
proceeded from the cellar. Two perfons went
down to examine, and found, in one corner of a
fmall tight room, a quantity of June cabbages, on
which the fun had fhone about three hours in a day.
They had rotted, and funk down in a lump of putrefaction. They run a ftick under them, and lift-
ed them up, and there immediately iffued fuch
an intolerable ftench, as obliged them inftantly to
leave the cellar. A vomiting was brought on at
once, which lafted them nearly an hour. Notwithftanding that the doors and windows of the cellar
were thrown open, it was two days before they
could clear it out. No other perfon in the family
was taken afterwards, and thofe who were already
feized foon recovered."

The malignant epidemic, or yellow fever, which
prevailed, in the fummer of 1797, in Providence,
Rhode-Ifland; in 1795, in Norfolk, Virginia;*
and, in 1791, in New-York, evidently took their
origin from gafes exhaled from vegetable and ani-

* Webfter's Collection, p. 148 & feq.

C

mal fubſtances, fuffered to collect and putrefy, on expoſure to a heated atmoſphere. It would be endleſs and unneceſſary to add facts in further confirmation of the noxious and deleterious qualities of certain gaſes, formed from vegetable and animal putrefaction, on its application to the conſtitution. Thoſe already related, as well as various other inſtances, fufficiently confirm, that the greateſt degree of vitiation which the atmoſphere manifeſts by its operation upon the conſtitution, proceeds from the effluvia emitted from certain vegetable and animal fubſtances during putrefaction. And, as far as the innumerable facts on this fubject have been collected and examined, there exiſts the moſt cogent evidence, that the products juſt named form infection, or contagion, marſh-miaſmata, or human effluvia, or whatever other name has been affixed to it. What the precife nature of thefe exhalations, or caufe of fevers, was, and which the particular noxious gas, though long a fubject of inquiry, remained unknown, till, within a few years fince, Mitchill, Profeſſor of Chemiſtry, Natural Hiſtory, and Agriculture, &c. in Columbia College, engaged in an inveſtigation of its properties, made known to the world what that poiſonous fomething, which is formed during animal and certain vegetable putrefaction, was. He difcovered it to be a portion of fepton (azote), one of the elements of the body undergoing putrefaction, united chemically with more or lefs of oxygene (the acidifying principle), in the form of feptic (nitric) oxyd and acid.* On

* Vide Mitchill on Contagion.

the formation and prefence of this compound, it is prefumed, do peftilential and other malignant dif-eafes depend. And, in proportion as a greater or lefs quantity of the above compound is formed; in proportion to its fparfe or concentrated ftate; in proportion to the length of time, the fufceptibility of the conftitution to be operated upon, and the circumftances under which it is applied; will the difeafes, depending upon this caufe, be more or lefs violent, and attended with various peftilential fymptoms.

## CHAPTER III.

*Inquiry into the Hiftory, Production, and Qualities, of that Acid which attends the Putrefaction of fuch Bodies as give Rife to malignant and peftilential Difeafes.*

SEPTON, the bafe of the acid of putrefaction, or feptic acid, is one of the moft abundant elements in nature: it has not hitherto been fubjected to any exa-mination by itfelf, as no experiments have been able to detect it in a diftinct and feparate ftate. In com-bination with caloric (the matter of heat,) it forms feptous (azotic) gas, which compofes nearly three fourths of our atmofphere, and is the fame fpecies of air which living plants are fuppofed to exhale in the night, according to Ingenhouz.* It likewife

* 2 Experiences fur, &c. fect. vii.

conſtitutes one of the elementary principles of certain plants : and, from the reſult of certain experiments made by Eagleton Smith, Eſq.* appears to be one of the elements which compoſe animal poiſons, as was, ſome time previous to this, preſumed by Profeſſor Mitchill. From the ſimilar action on animals, of ſuch animal poiſons as were uſed by the experimentor, ſuch as that of bees, ants, and ſome other inſects, with the decoction of the poiſonous plants, laurel, tobacco, digitalis, opium, &c. it appears highly probable, that their deleterious qualities are owing to a modification of this ſame principle, viz. ſepton. It alſo enters largely into the compoſition of the muſcular fibre, blood, and lean parts of animals, in combination with carbone, hydrogene, and phoſphorus, which are united together by a certain portion of oxygene, forming animal oxyds and acids, in proportion to the degree of oxygenation. This gas, in its pure and diſtinct form, is incapable to ſupport reſpiration and combuſtion; while it ſuſtains the life of plants, which appear to poſſeſs the power of decompounding it, and to attach to themſelves the ſepton, which enters into and conſtitutes one of their principles.† This principle, or element, is alſo capable of uniting with oxygene, the principle of acidity, forming with it, in proportion to the quantity of this laſt ſubſtance, 1. The gaſeous oxyd of ſepton (dephlogiſticated nitrous air); 2. Septic (nitrous) gas; 3 and 4. Septous

---

* Vide Appendix A.
† Mitchill on Manures. Med. Repoſ. vol. i. No. 1.

and feptic (nitrous and nitric) acids; and, 5. Septic acid gas.

1. In the firft of thefe forms, that of the gafeous oxyd, in which the acidifying principle is fo fmall as not to manifeft the fmalleft degree of acidity, it is capable of fupporting combuftion, but is highly deleterious to the lives of animals, which it deftroys the moment they are furrounded by an atmofphere of this kind.* 2 and 3. The next degree of combination of oxygene with fepton, is the feptic gas, and the feptous acid. Thefe are artificial productions, and never found to exift in the atmofphere for any confiderable length of time, as their exiftence depends on being kept clofed, and free from contact with the air. The rapidity with which they abforb oxygene from the atmofphere, on expofure, is fo great as to become quickly faturated with this principle, and turn to feptic acid. As their exiftence in the air is only momentary, unlefs kept from coming in contact with it, they can have no material influence on man or brute animals; and their qualities are fo widely different from thofe of the more highly oxygenated form, the experiments and conclufions drawn from the two former, cannot apply to account for the phenomena of the latter. 4 and 5. The feptic acid, which is ftill higher dofed with oxygene, and the feptic acid gas, the higheft degree of oxygenation of fepton, the form in which thefe compounds moft commonly exift, and which are produced wherever fepton and oxygene

---

* Prieftley on Air, vol. ii. p. 35.

come into chemical union, have, for a length of time, been confidered of *mineral* origin, and claffed among the acids of this kingdom. How far this opinion is founded in experience, and deduced from facts, will appear on examination of the materials, and fources, from whence it is derived. It is well known that nitre confifts of feptic acid joined to pot-afh, and is ufually formed during the decay of animal and fuch vegetable bodies as contain fepton. And it is afcertained, that fepton and oxygene enter into the compofition of thofe fubftances, when alive, and have gone into new combinations, on their difengagement, after death. One of thefe recent compounds muft be feptous and feptic acid, conftituting, by junction with a faline bafe, the feptite of pot-afh. The theory of falt-petre thus neceffarily prefumes the generation of feptous and feptic acid, from two of the elements difengaged from organic texture. And as fepton, the radical of the acid, is efpecially abundant in animal bodies, there is little difficulty in comprehending both how, in fuch circumftances, it attracts the acidifying principle, and afterwards attaches itfelf to the alkali. Nicholfon obferves it to be well known, that the feptous acid, inftead of exifting in the mineral kingdom, is almoft always produced by a concurrence of circumftances, chiefly confifting in the expofure of putrefying fubftances to the atmofphere; and that it is formed by the union of two principles, which are always found in atmofpheric air, and the exhalations of putrefying fub-

ftances.*　The nitrous quality of the earths at the
bottom of graves, in which animal diſorganization
has taken place, is further teſtimony of the origin
of this acid, as in this caſe it could not have acquired its ſeptic quality from any other ſource.
Hence may be underſtood how other earths, ſuch
as thoſe of ſtables, cow-houſes, cellars, vaults, drains,
ſinks, &c. &c. acquire their nitrous quality. During the putrefactive proceſs of ſuch vegetable bodies as contain ſepton, and animal matter, which
abounds in this principle, the oxygene derived either from the corrupting bodies themſelves, from
the water in or near them, or from the atmoſphere,
unites with this principle, and forms the ſeptic acid,
which, being taken up by theſe earths, converts
them into nitrous ſoils.

In further confirmation of the origin of this acid,
may be added the authority of Fourcroi, who ſays,
" It is no longer to be doubted that the ſalt-petre,
which forms itſelf under our eyes, in ſoils ſoaked
by vegetable and animal juices, or in ſtones impregnated with the ſame juices, or their vapour, (the
materials which compoſe the floors and walls of our
ſtables, vaults, &c.) repreſent, in this reſpect, real
artificial nitre-beds."†

This acid is alſo found to exiſt occaſionally in
the atmoſphere. The experiments of Margraff‡
on ſnow and rain-water, and Bergman's analyſis of
waters, prove its preſence in the air, from whence

* Nicholſon's Chemiſtry, p. 32.
† Vide Med. Repoſ. vol. i. No. 1. p. 71.
‡ Vide Watſon's Chem. Eſſays, vol. ii. p. 79.

they are precipitated by thefe bodies, and mix with them in their defcent. The nitrous quality of the calcareous matter of old walls, which takes place to fuch an extent as to be converted to economical purpofes, affords like proof of its prefence in the atmofphere.

The bafes of the two gafes, fepton and oxygene, which compofe this acid, conftitute likewife our atmofphere, but in different proportions and combinations. The feptic acid is found to contain four parts of oxygene and one of fepton, chemically united; while the proportion of thefe ingredients in atmofpheric air about the mean ratio, are 27 of the former to 73 of the latter; not, however, chemically united, but only diffufed through each other, as clay is diffufed through water, or as motes are feen paffing through fun-beams. Thefe gafeous components of the atmofphere are intimately blended, and mixed together, but do not lofe their attraction for caloric, by which they are continued in this ftate, and for which, in ordinary circumftances, they have a greater affinity feparately than for each other. It is by virtue of this attraction for the matter of heat, that they are each kept in a ftate of gas, and not fuffered to unite, and form feptic acid, and thereby deftroy the refpirability of the atmofphere.

Dr. Beddoes remarks, that " the nice balance of attraction between the conftituent parts of the atmofphere deferves notice. Thefe two fubftances, when clofely united, form nitrous (feptous) acid; if, therefore, they were not, by fome circumftances, prevented from uniting clofely, all the oxygene, with part of the azote (fepton), would be changed into a highly concentrated acid, and the waters of our globe would be converted into aqua-fortis," (feptous acid).* Fourcroi alfo obferves, " that this (feptic) acid is compofed of the fame elements with atmofpheric air, only under a different form, and in different proportions, from thofe which conftitute the atmofphere. Thefe facts are indifputably eftablifhed by experiments in which the nitric (feptic) acid is decompofed, and again produced by the union of the original elements. Hence it is demonftrated, that it confifts of four parts of oxygene, and one of azote (fepton). But thefe two principles, as contributing to the formation of the atmofphere, are in the proportion of a little more than two parts and one half of the firft, and one of the fecond, and exift in an uncombined ftate, feparately diffolved in a common menftruum, and without the poffibility of contracting a real chemical union. Hence it arifes, that atmofpheric air is never fpontaneoufly converted into nitric (feptic) acid."†

The formation of feptic acid in the atmofphere feems, however, to take place under certain circumftances; as when the two conftituent elements of the acid are brought into clofe union, and within the fphere of each other's attraction, by fome violent concuffions, fuch as lightning in thunder-ftorms. The experiments made by Mr. Cavendifh,‡ who,

* Confiderations on the Medicinal Ufe, and on the Productions, of Factitious Airs, p. 18.
† Vide Med. Repof. vol. i. No. 1. p. 68 and 69.
‡ Chaptal's Chem. vol i. p. 219.

by paffing the electric fpark through a portion of oxygenous and feptous (azotic) gafes, obtained this acid, further tends to corroborate this opinion, and leads, at leaft, to a belief, that this procefs, to a larger amount, is conftantly taking place in the upper regions of our atmofphere, by the intervention of the electric matter.

---

## CHAPTER IV.

*Action of this Acid and its Oxyds upon Timber, Metals, Earths, alkaline Salts, and Water.*

THE feptic acid having been fhewn, in the preceding chapter, to owe its origin to animal and vegetable decompofition, its operation on timber, metals, &c. will next be confidered.

Facts, fufficiently numerous, prove that this acid, generated by putrefaction, is always on or near the furface of the earth, and from thence, when exifting in any confiderable quantity, pervades the atmofphere, and, on meeting with certain bodies, unites with them, and becomes fixed or decompounded. If, in its vaporific form, it meets with the woody portion of dwellings, around and in which it is more or lefs plentifully evolved, more efpecially the unclean, there can be no doubt but a quantity of this acid is imbibed, as all thefe materials are porous in a greater or lefs degree. There are no direct experiments, however, which prove

that there exifts a chemical union between the acid
and it; but, from the readinefs with which wood
is penetrated by water, and the known union which
this latter body poffeffes for contagion, it muft not
unfrequently be conveyed in this manner, and combined with the timber of human habitations, where
thefe gafeous vapours, extricated during vegetable
and animal putrefaction, abound: the quantity
taken up will, in all probability, be proportionate
to the porofity of their texture; and in this ratio
may the different kinds of wood be capable of im-
bibing the acid. The rapid decay and rotting of
the timber of fuch veffels as carry wheat, is further
teftimony of the union and deftructive operation
of this acid, on its application to wood. The manner in which this procefs takes place, appears to be
owing to the grain falling through the flooring of
the veffel, where, on mixing with the water there
commonly prefent, putrefies.

Wheat, containing the principle of putrefaction
in no fmall quantity, has, during its diffolution,
this principle, united with a fufficiency of the oxygene, fupplied either by the water, or what it itfelf
contained, to form the feptic acid, which, fpread-
ing itfelf, attaches and unites with the timber,
caufing it to rot and decay, more or lefs rapidly, in
proportion to the ftrength and activity which the
acid attains.

From this difpofition of the acid of putrefaction
to combine and unite with the woody portions of
dwellings, fhips, or whatever elfe it comes in contact with, may it happen, that the noxious matter,

faid, in fome veffels, to infect each fucceffive crew, derives its poifon.

2. The operation of the feptic acid, as above observed, in rotting and breaking down the timber of veffels, has been noticed to ruft and corrode, proportionally quick, fuch iron fpikes and nails as were expofed, in a fimilar manner, to the fame caufe; and, from its corrofive qualities, gradually deftroys and wears them away, if prefent in fufficient quantity, till nothing but ruft is left remaining. Such inftances as have been collected and examined on this fubject, go to prove this operation of the acid on metals. It has been obferved, that in the Weft-India Iflands, where putrefaction goes on rapidly, fuch iron cannon as were expofed to the atmofphere, commonly furcharged more or lefs with this acid, rufted much fooner than thofe which had been buried in the fand in falt water. The teftimony of Van Sweiten alfo corroborates the activity and deftructive influence of this acid on metallic bodies. He mentions, that at Oczakow, during the plague, " the inftruments made ufe of by the furgeons turned as black and livid as if they had been dipped in aqua-fortis," (feptous acid)—and " the filver hilt of a fword, which, all the time of the plague, hung up in a tent, was changed quite black."

3. The action of this acid, in refpect to earths, is more obferved, and takes place to a larger extent. It readily unites with calcareous earth (lime), whenever they come within chemical attraction, in the form of a feptite of the fame, (calcareous nitre,) as appears from the nitrous quality of old walls of

privies, finks, drains, &c. Grounds frequently trod-
den by cattle, and impregnated with their excre-
ments, the walls of flaughter-houfes, and the like,
where exhalations from putrid animal and vegetable fubftances abound, as well as the formation of
nitrous earths at the bottom of graves in which animal bodies have decayed, puts it beyond difpute,
that thefe earths have an attraction for and unite
with this acid. This affinity between the acid of
putrefaction and lime, takes place to a greater or
lefs extent in every habitation, more efpecially in
large and crowded cities, where the ftricteft attention is not paid to remove all filth, and putrefying
animal and vegetable materials. It was fo well
known, as to become an object worthy the attention of a body corporate in Paris, who obtained li-
cence to take away as much of the old mortar of
the walls of houfes, torn down, as they pleafed, for
the exprefs purpofe of making nitre. Hence may
be learned the quantities of feptic poifon that is
prefent, and floats about the habitations of man,
gradually undermining his conftitution, and caufing malignant difeafes, if not taken out of circulation, and combined with fome fubftance.

4. This acid likewife, on meeting with the carbonates of alkaline falts, decompofes them, by de-
ftroying the chemical affinity fubfifting between
them and the weaker acids; while, at the fame
time, it attaches to itfelf the alkaline bafis, forming
with it a feptite of the fame. The facts already
quoted, in the firft chapter, put it beyond doubt,
that the acid of putrefaction readily unites with

pot-afh, foda, and ammonia, refpectively, in the form of feptites, wherever they come within the fphere of each other's attraction: and, if it is evident that thefe bodies enter into combination, there will be no difficulty to fhew, that this acid likewife unites with fuch falts as have an alkali for their bafe. According to Bergman's tables of elective attractions, the feptic (nitric) acid has a greater affinity for pot-afh than for any other alkali; and that no acid but the fulphuric will diffolve their union.* On coming, therefore, in contact with fuch falts as have this alkali for their bafis, it will decompofe them, and, from its fuperior affinity for this latter fubftance, combine with it in the form of a feptite of pot-afh. In the fame manner will thofe falts, having foda and ammonia for their bafis, be operated upon by this acid.

5. The prefence of this acid in water, and its ready and entire mifcibility with this body, is evident from the experiments made, with the utmoft diligence and attention, by Bergman and other chemifts, on rain and fnow water. The teftimony of Lewis is further confirmation of this union between the two bodies. He obferves, that " common waters, both atmofpherical and fubterraneous, contain a little of this acid in combination with it ;"† and

---

* Although the feptic acid does not poffefs an attraction for either of the alkalies, in fo eminent a degree as the fulphuric, according to Bergman's tables of elective attractions, yet, from his note, it appears it is capable to difengage the fulphuric acid, in fome cafes, partially, from its connection with alkalies, though not fo rapid and entirely as either of the other acids.

† Materia Medica, vol. ii. p. 120.

that among the fubflances commonly found in waters, is the " nitrous (feptous) acid, combined with
an alkali into nitre, or with fome of the foluble
earths into nitrous falts."* " The pureft of the
common waters is that of fnow; and the faline matter of this kind of water is commonly of the nitrous
kind, compofed of the acid of nitre (feptic acid),
united with calcareous earth."

It is agreed upon by almoft all obfervers, that
the vapours from ftagnant waters do feldom occafion much mifchief, as long as the mud and flime
remain covered. The reafon of this is obvioufly
owing to the mud, while covered by the water,
emitting its poifon but flowly, which, as it arifes
to the furface, mixes with the incumbent water,
and remains united with it, fo that little or none
efcapes to taint the atmofphere. But at length,
as evaporation goes on, and the water is nearly eva-
porated, thefe fluids, rarefied by heat, and becoming volatile, afcend into the atmofphere, and taint
it with their noxious qualities, to the detriment of
man and brute animals, who live and move in it.
On this mifcibility of feptic, or acid of putrefaction, with water, no doubt, does it happen, that
fhowers of rain, as obferved by almoft every writer
on the difeafes of hot climates, poffefs fuch beneficial and falutary effects. The rain, in its defcent,
meets with this acid, unites with it, and thus pre-
cipitates it again to the earth, leaving the atmofphere in a ftate freed from its poifon. In the fame

* Vol. i. p. 118.

manner may dews and fogs, in their defcent, unite
with this acid vapour; and to the gradual and flow
precipitation of water from the air, falling through
this infectious fluid, and carrying a portion of contagion along with it, does it happen, that the crews
of veffels, fent on fhore, and fleeping on or near the
furface of the earth, in the open air, in fuch places
where thefe peftilential vapours abound, are fo commonly feized with difeafes which deftroy their lives.
The natives of the Eaft-Indies are fo well aware of
the noxious qualities, at times, of rain-water, which
falls firft in fhowers, that they are cautious how
they expofe themfelves to it. As evidence of this
atmofpherical water containing fomething deleterious, it has been known to caufe foal-leather to
become mouldy and rotten in the fpace of forty-
eight hours. The fame was alfo obferved to happen in our own city, in the time of the epidemic, in
1795. Hunter alfo remarks, that expofure to rain
is believed to be the caufe of fevers in the ifland of
Jamaica. The practice among Europeans at Con-
ftantinople, Grand-Cairo, and other places where
the plague rages, to cleanfe all their goods, &c.
they receive by means of water, is further corrobo-
ration that peftilential gas unites with water, info-
much that thefe bodies, thus cleanfed, are deprived
of communicating any poifon they had previoufly
imbibed. To this mifcibility of contagious fluids
with water, may cold bathing, in malignant difeafes, owe its beneficial and falutary effects—the
poifon which adhered to the fkin and its pores being

thereby conveyed off, and rendered harmlefs to the conftitution.

From the preceding facts, then, it may be concluded, that the feptic acid, generated in all filthy and unclean dwellings, finks, &c. on meeting with either of the fubftances above enumerated, unites with them, becomes fixed or decompounded, and thus taken out of circulation. By this wife provifion of nature, the acid of putrefaction, which muft be formed in no fmall quantity, confidering the immenfe and incalculable mafs of vegetable and animal matter which is continually undergoing diforganization; is arrefted and reftrained from affuming its corrofive, ftimulant, and poifonous qualities, which it exerts on man and brute animals, when fet loofe in the atmofphere.

---

## CHAPTER V.

*Effects produced by it upon the Conftitution of Men, particularly the Mouth, Throat, Alimentary Canal, exterior and pulmonic Surface, Heart, Blood-veffels, and Lymphatic Syftem.*

HAVING afcertained, as it is hoped, the caufe of moft endemic and epidemic difeafes, the fources of their origin and formation, together with their affinities and action on different bodies; their effects on the living conftitution fhall next be confidered.

E

ɪ and 2. The effects of oxyds and acids of this sort, when applied to the living body, which, in some instances, may be completely surrounded by an atmosphere-highly charged with these gaseous fluids, are inflammations or ulcerations, together with many other diseases of different kinds; and, if inspired in a concentrated state, may cause instantaneous death. On its application to the fauces and throat, from its caustic and corroding nature, it may inflame, and excite heat and distressing pain in the surrounding parts, and bring on apthæ, and erythematic affections of the pharynx and æsophagus, as is observed to happen under certain circumstances where it is generated, or present, from any other cause, in sufficient quantity. The experiments of Professor Mitchill,* in his course of lectures, in 1796, on the tartar of the teeth, shews that this acid may be (and is occasionally present in the mouth) either formed from the remains of corrupting food, or taken in, by inspiration, with atmospheric air. This operation and effect, produced by the acid and its oxyd, on the fauces and throat, is further confirmed by facts of diseases of these parts, induced by breathing air highly vitiated with pestilential effluvia. To this effect is the observation of Huxham, who remarks, that " for many months past we had scarce the slightest fever, but it was attended with sore-throat, apthæ, and some kind of cuticular eruption, and that, too, in pleuritic and pneumonic diforders; so greatly did the constitu-

* Vide Mitchill's letter to Thomas Charles Hope, M. D. in the New York Mag. for February, 1797.

tion of the air, &c. feem difpofed to produce eruptions in all forts of feyerifh indifpofitions."*

Robertfon, in his remarks on the Monthly Review of the fick in July and May, alfo obferves, that to the clafs of fever, the dyfenteric belly-ache, and almoft all the cough and fore-throat cafes, fhould be added, becaufe they originated, I had nearly faid, from the fame fource; thefe different appearances depending on the habits or conftitutions of the fubjects infected."†

In the peftilential fever which prevailed at Winchefter Hofpital, many were feized with uneafinefs of fwallowing, and complained of a forenefs of the throat.‡ To this may be added the authority of Chifholm, who, in his account of an epidemic fever in Grenada, remarks, among other obfervations, that " fome complained of a rawnefs, as it were, from the throat to the ftomach;" or, as they exprefſed it, " a rawnefs and burning of their inwards."§

Hence, then, it will appear, that this volatile acid does occafionally enter the fauces, and extends its influence to the æfophagus, caufing a greater or lefs degree of inflammation and uneafinefs in the parts, according as the poifon is in a more or lefs concentrated form, and to the length of time it is applied. The mucus which lubricates the parts, and is continually excreted in confiderable quanti-

* On Fevers, p. 274.
† On Jail Fevers, p. 325.
‡ Smyth on Jail Fever, p. 12.
§ Med. Com. for 1792, p. 267.

ties, more efpecially on the introduction of any ex-
traneous body, may, in all probability, defend them
from more repeated attacks of this acid, by uniting
with, and preventing its coming in contact with the
parts.

3. The operation of this acid on the ftomach
and inteftines appears more frequent than the above,
and is productive of greater evils and fatality to the
conftitution. It may be either taken into the ftomach
by mixing with the faliva, and fwallowed, or may be
generated in the inteftinal canal, on the putrefaction of fome of thofe fubftances that are taken in for
our nourifhment. The opinions of the moft re-
fpectable authorities countenance thefe modes of
operation. The faliva and fluids of the mouth
confift principally of water, and may, therefore, be
fuppofed to poffefs an attraction for thefe contagious gafes. The infection, thus finding its way into
the mouth, will almoft unavoidably get into the
ftomach during the deglutition of our food, or be
conveyed there with our drink.

Balfour, in a Treatife on Putrid Inteftinal Remitting Fevers, afcribes the caufes of thefe complaints to a putrid ftate of the *mucus lining the inteftines*, which, being abforbed by the lacteal veffels,
and carried into the blood, caufes the febrile ftate.
—" This mucus receives the infection firft by contagious matter taken into the ftomach by means of
the faliva."*

To this may be added the authorities of Turner,

* Page 130.

Gardiner, and Lind; the latter of whom says, that swallowing the spittle, in infected places, is justly deemed a means of sooner acquiring the taint; for which reason neither the nurses, nor any one else, should be suffered to eat in infected hospitals. " I am apt to think, that infection, from whatever impure fountain it is derived, does first discover itself by affecting the stomach and intestines."*

Another mode in which the diseases depending on the septic acid are generated, is by the putrefaction of those substances taken into the stomach, from time to time, for our support. If it is evident, that animal and vegetable matter, undergoing dissolution in the open air, give rise to the septic acid and its oxyds, is it not presumable, that this same compound will be formed, on the corruption of similar substances, in the *primæ viæ* of human bodies? It is necessary to the maintenance of life, that a proper quantity of food be taken into the stomach, from time to time; and that the digestive organs perform their functions properly; for, as the diet is principally of the animal kind, and, consequently, containing all the elements necessary to the formation of the septic compounds, it would undergo putrefaction in the intestinal canal, were it not prevented by the saliva, gastric liquor, pancreatic juice, and bile, which, mixing with it, dissolve and prepare it for the various purposes it is intended to answer. As long, then, as the stomach secretes its liquors in healthy and due

* On Hot Climates, p. 65.

quantities, will its contents be kept in utter impof-
fibility of forming the feptic poifon. But when
thefe preventatives are entirely fufpended, or weak-
ened, from debilitating caufes, fuch as the too libe-
ral ufe of fpirituous liquors, exceffive heat, fatigue,
or from any other procefs by which its healthy functions are deftroyed or impaired, then it is evident
that the food will be liable to corrupt, and the
products formed from thefe materials, within the
ftomach and inteftines, fimilar to thofe which obtain without the body. A fource of poifonous effluvia feems thus to exift in our bodies ; and, from
its ftimulant qualities, the occurrence of naufea,
burning pain, and exceffive vomiting, together with
other fymptoms of gaftretis, will not be difficult of
explanation. To this caufe, whether generated in
the *primæ viæ*, or taken in from a vitiated atmofphere, when applied to the inteftinal canal, are di-
arrhœas, dyfenteries, and cholera morbus, difeafes
of the fame genus, only differently modified, refera-
ble. The inflamed ftate of the ftomach, duode-
num, and lower parts of the inteftinal canal, and
the black gangrenous and mortified fpots, are all
owing to the operation of this acid, which, in fome
cafes, may acquire a higher degree of malignancy
than common, by uniting with a larger portion of
cxygene. The coffee-coloured matter, commonly
called *black vomit*, ejected in what are called *bilious*
*remitting* fevers, feems to owe its colour to a mixture
of this acid, as appears from its ftimulant nature,
noticed by diffectors, with a quantity of bile and
blood, which is poured out of fuch veffels as have

their coats deftroyed by this poifon. That this is not a difcharge of putrid bile, is evident from the experiments of Saunders, who obferved, that fo far from its becoming putrid, it was lefs liable to undergo this procefs than any other of the animal fluids, arid would even prevent the diforganization of fuch fubftances as were immerfed in it.* Blood, mixed with bile, became putrid in three days; while no mark of putrefaction manifefted itfelf in the bile till the fixth day.✝ Hence alfo it is evident, that putrid bile, which has been affigned as the caufe of bilious fevers, has no agency in its production; for if the bile did, in reality, become putrid, this change muft neceffarily have previoufly taken place in the blood, in which ftate the animal muft expire within a few moments after putrefaction takes place.

4. On the application of thefe peftilential fluids, which have been confidered the caufes of the difeafes mentioned, to the bodies of men, which it may completely furround in fome cafes, is it prefumed, are the various eruptions and petechiæ, fo common in fevers of the worft type, to be explained; and not often to be referred to critical depofitions of humors from the blood. Thefe affections will put on different appearances and malignancy, in proportion to the concentrated ftate of the poifon, the conftitution, and parts to which it is applied. From the difpofition of this acid to adhere to bed-clothes

---

* On the Liver, p. 130.
✝ On the Liver, p. 110.

and bedding, of which there are innumerable inftances, it will readily appear how thefe peftilential
eruptions are produced, efpecially on thofe parts
that are kept conftantly covered, as the back, loins,
&c. which are thus continually furrounded by an
atmofphere of contagious vapours. The fkin, thus
befet by this fluid, whofe particles feem to inhere
in its pores, becomes inflamed, and puts on this
morbid appearance. The yellow colour of the
fkin, in fome cafes of 'highly contagious difeafes,
feems to depend upon the fame caufe, and not to
an abforption of bile, as has been fuppofed by writers on bilious remitting fevers. If thefe changes
of colour in the fkin were really owing to abforbed
or to regurgitated bile, the colour of the urine, in
thefe cafes, ought to be deeply tinged with this fluid,
and the fæces to put on an afh-coloured appearance,
as in jaundice; but none of thefe appearances are
obferved to take place in the fevers where this
pretended abforption is alledged. Befide, it is well
known, that fuch parts of the fkin to which this
poifon is artificially applied, will put on a yellow appearance, refembling that which is obferved to take
place in what is called *yellow* fever. It has been
obferved, that perfons fick with this fever, which
had been taken in the Weft-Indies, had that part
of their eyes which was, in vifion, expofed to
atmofpheric air, tinged with yellow; while the re-
mainder of the eye retained its natural colour. In
this cafe the eye could not have acquired this
colour from an abforption of bile; which, if it
had been the cafe, would alfo have been evident in

other parts of the eye and body. Were it not, pro-
bably, for the perpetual fupply of tears, which wafh
the eyes, and thus convey off any contagious fluids
that may be applied, thefe appearances might of-
tener occur, as impreffions would be quicker obferved in this organ than on the fkin.

5. This acid, in a vaporific form, does, no doubt,
fometimes enter the trachea, with the air, in refpiration, where it may inflame and deftroy the parts
with which it comes in contact; and, in its paffage to
the lungs, if in a concentrated form, may occafion
fudden death. In this manner may the fudden ex-
tinction of life, in perfons expofed to the contagion
of the plague, as obferved by Ruffel, be accounted
for.*　If this gafeous fluid be infpired in fuch a di-
luted ftate as not to occafion immediate death, it
may caufe catarrhal affections, anxiety, coma, fuf-
focation, &c. depending on the fparfe or concentrated form, and circumftances under which it is
applied. When mixed with atmofpheric air, and
taken into the lungs, it will not ferve the purpofes
of refpiration, as but a fmall portion of vital air will
be decompounded, owing to the large quantity of
non-refpirable air which is taken in. The heat of
the body muft thereby be leffened, and the con-
tractions of the heart and arteries become more
flow and feeble. In this way may the purple and
blackifh fpots of perfons dead of fever, occafioned by this acid and its oxyd, and the livid
and dark colour of the fkin, attended with

* Hiftory of Aleppo, p. 233.

F

coldnefs during life, be accounted for; the lungs not being able to reftore to the fyftem its ufual and neceffary fupply of oxygene. Hæmorrhages, debility, and proftration of ftrength, together with want of cohefion in the folids, might all be explained upon the fame principle, the mufcles being deprived of their ufual quantity of oxygene, and overcharged with fepton.

6. If this acid be formed in the ftomach and inteftines, or taken in by the faliva, and applied to the mouth, fauces, cuticular and pulmonic furface, can it be fuppofed, that it fhould not be taken up by the abforbent veffels of the fkin and pulmonic organs, or abforbed by the lacteals of the inteftines, which are known, in fome inftances, even to take up fome of the fæces, and carried into the mafs of blood? That fomething of a peftilential nature is conveyed into the blood, appears from the evident marks of peftilential infection, which children, born of mothers fick with the plague, bring along with them. Whether they acquired this taint immediately from the blood circulating through the umbilical cord, or from the *liquor amnii*, or both conjoined, is immaterial to our prefent purpofe, as, in either manner, it goes to prove what has been faid above. The acid fweats thrown out from the poifoned mafs of blood, by means of the fmall exhalent arteries, in malignant and peftilential difeafes, forming the matter of contagion, and adhering to the bed-clothes and linen, which, by its corrofive qualities, it deftroys and rots; and, if excreted in any confiderable quantity, fo commonly re-

lieves the patient; inafmuch as the volume of poifon contained in the arterial fyftem is thereby leffened; fhews that the blood, in certain difeafes, con-
tains fomething of a noxious nature. The appearances alfo which blood, drawn in peftilential fevers,
puts on, correfpond with that in which feptic gas
had been artifically injected.* Blood, thus infected
with this poifon, taken up by the abforbent veffels,
will be carried the round of circulation, and will
continue to ftimulate the heart and arteries, wear-
ing out their excitability, and, confequently, bring
on death, if the conftitution is incapable of becoming habituated to its ftimulus, or part, or whole, of
the ftimulus be not fubducted. If it be prefent in
any great quantity, it may caufe a fudden extinc-
tion of the vital principle, as is obferved fometimes
to happen in highly peftilential difeafes.

7. The above-mentioned compounds, when abforbed by the lymphatics, may inflame them, and
caufe obftructions, indurations, and even fuppuration, of thofe glands through which they pafs, as is
commonly obferved to take place in the inguinal
and axillary glands, in the plague, and other difeafes produced by a peftilential ftate of the atmofphere, where it is abforbed in a highly concentrated
form. Inftances have occurred, where the lymphatics of the hand, on this extremity being wounded,
in diffecting bodies, in which the feptic acid appears
already to be formed, were highly inflamed, and

* Vide Mitchill on the effects of contagion on the heart, in the New-
York Mag. for 1796.

could be readily traced from the part where this fluid had been applied, in their courfe to the glands in the axilla, in which fubfequent fuppuration took place. Befide the affections of thefe glands, thofe of the mefentery will be liable to like ailments; and more frequently, as this deleterious fluid will be more frequently applied to them, by reafon of its abforption from the inteftines. The feptic compounds, paffing through the lacteals, will inflame them, and extend to the glands, in their way to the thoracic duct, and bring on an indurated or fchirrous ftate : if it be abforbed in a highly concentrated ftate, it may alfo communicate its effects to the mefentery. When thefe glands become indurated or inflamed, the chyle will neceffarily be obftructed totally, or in part, in its circulation through thefe glands ; confequently the fyftem will not receive a fupply of nourifhment equal to the quantity expended in performing its healthy functions. Hence the body muft wafte away, and the difeafe named marafmus be induced. The frequent dropfical affections which follow long-continued intermittents, dyfenteries, and other difeafes of the fame clafs, appear, in many inftances, to be owing to obftructions of thefe glands, which do not allow a free paffage to the lymph, which is therefore depofited in the different cavities and cellular texture of the body; and in proportion as the obftruction is more or lefs univerfal, will the difeafe be general or local.

# CHAPTER VI.

*Application of this Principle to explain the Preven-*
*tion and Destruction of Infection, or Contagion, in*
*Ships performing Quarantine, in Jails, Hospitals,*
*private Dwellings, in regulating the Police of Ci-*
*ties, in the Management of Lazarettos, &c.*

HAVING shewn the operation of the septic
acid, on its application to the constitution, we come
next to consider its prevention and destruction in
ships, performing quarantine, &c. &c.

1. In such ships as have these noxious effluvia
floating about, either derived from articles infected,
or generated from the collection and putrefaction
of such materials as contain septon, it will be proper, from the known affinity which subsists between
these contagious vapours and calcareous earth
(lime), to expose this substance to an atmosphere
thus impregnated. White-washing between decks,
and all such places as may admit of this practice,
will therefore be the most advantageous method in
which it can be applied, as a larger surface will
thereby be exposed, and, consequently, a greater
portion of the acid taken up and neutralized in a
given time. Frequent repetitions of this practice
will be necessary where the contagion is abundant,
as the lime will become saturated with this principle, and incapable to attract and take out of circulation any more of the noxious compound. In
such instances where these effluvia have, for any

length of time, been prefent in veffels, it is more
than probable, that from the capability exifting between the two to unite, the timber of the latter
may imbibe fome of thefe vapours; and to this, as
has been above remarked, may it be owing, that
the fucceffive crews of certain veffels are fometimes
deftroyed. To deftroy this connection between
thefe two bodies, as well as to prevent the future
afcent of the gas, and thus again taint the circumambient atmofphere, a folution of the vegetable
alkali (pot-afh), in water, which poffeffes the greateft
known affinity for this fluid, will be a proper pre-
ventative. It will difengage the acid from its connection with the wood, in confequence of this fuperior attraction, and join with it itfelf. Frequent
wafhing the apartments will likewife tend greatly
to cleanfe and carry off the noxious vapours; and
will alfo, by being imbibed into the texture of the
wood, fet loofe and convey away fuch poifon as may
remain. Ventilation muft not be neglected: the
contaminated atmofphere will thereby have part of
its volume conveyed off, and a quantity of purer
air admitted; thus rendering its ftimulating quality
lefs violent and active.

2. The fame means, recommended above, for
the deftruction of thefe fluids in fhips, will apply
to jails.—As white-wafhing the walls with lime can
at all times and readily be done here, it ought, from
time to time, to be renewed; the poifonous effluvia
being thus conftantly taken up, and rendered harmlefs. Wafhing the apartments with water or ley,
which has a ftill greater affinity for thefe effluvia, will

disengage the poison which they so commonly become impregnated with, to the injury of the health of
the inhabitants of these places. In no one instance
will it be more necessary to admit fresh air, than in
these places. The pent up vapours will, in a short
time, acquire a high degree of malignancy, and
cause difficulty of respiration, uneasiness about the
precordia, and bring on other symptoms indicative
of a vitiated state of the atmosphere.

3. The regulation of hospitals will be answered
by the same means already noticed for jails and
ships : but, from the specific gravity of this acid or
its oxyd, it will occupy the lowermost parts of the
rooms. " Under an atmospheric pressure which
supports the quick-silver in the barometer at 29.
84 inches, and in a temperature of 54. 5 of Fahren-
heit, a cubic foot of azotic gas weighed one ounce,
thirty grains and one half; and of oxygenous gas,
one ounce, one drachm, and fifty-one grains : it
is presumable that a combination of the two, that
is, thirty-seven parts of oxygene united to thirty-
three of azote, would form a fluid of nearly the
same weight with atmospheric air, or rather heavier;
and the probability of this would increase, by con-
sidering that a cubic foot of nitrous gas, which con-
tains only thirty-one parts more of oxygene than
the gaseous oxyd does, weighs one ounce, two
drachms, and thirty-nine grains." Hence, then,
persons who lay on or near the floor, where this
compound is present, will suffer more than those
who walk through these places; and for this reason
also will the atmosphere on the second floor be

more refpirable than that on the firft, or loweft.
Vent-holes, upon a level with the lowermoft part
of the room, may therefore more readily fuffer the
efcape of thefe noxious compounds; and, in addition with thofe fubftances that take up and neutralize them quickly, reftore the purity and refpirability of the air.

4. The preventatives already mentioned, particularly for fhips, which may be confidered as floating habitations of men, will alfo apply to the cleanfing and purification of private dwellings. From
what has been faid on the affinity of lime with the
feptic acid, it will, at firft view, appear how much
more preferable, and conducive to the health of
the inhabitants, fuch dwellings, which have their
walls plaiftered with this fubftance, will be, to thofe
of gypfum (fulphate of lime), which is incapable to
neutralize the acid. The common practice to prevent and deftroy contagion in private dwellings, by
means of alkalies diffolved in water, fuch as ley,
&c. and lime, fhews how much preferable this management and contrivance is to that of burning tar,
coal, fulphur, &c. fubftances that poffefs no ufe-
ful, but pernicious qualities, inafmuch as the peftilential matter refifts the attractive powers of thefe
fubftances. (Vide fect. vii).

5. In regulating the police of cities, it will, at
firft view, appear highly neceffary, in order to prevent the formation of thefe noxious fluids, to remove all the materials, fuch as animal and certain
vegetable fubftances, from which they are generated.
In addition to the preventatives enumerated for the

prevention and deſtruction of contagion in jails, &c. planting trees along the ſtreets, eſpecially thoſe which are, from ſituation, more liable to collections of gaſes of this kind, will be of ſervice in decompounding theſe fluids, as ſoon as formed, if in conſiderable quantities, and thus reſtore the air to its former ſtate of reſpirability. " Theſe very ſubſtances (putrefying bodies and ſtreet-manure), that cauſe ſo much miſchief and terror in *cities*, are ſought after with great avidity by farmers, who purchaſe them at a high price, and uſe them, with much advantage, to fertilize their fields. The beneficial and ſalutary effects of this practice in huſbandry, makes it look as if nitrous acid and nitrous airs were good manures, and that vegetables had the power of decompounding them. That, in ſhort, in the economy of plants, there is a proceſs by which the ſepton and oxygene of theſe infectious fluids are ſeparated; and while the former remains in the vegetable as a part of its nutriment, the ſurpluſage of the latter, after forming gum, mucus, meal, &c. and other vegetable oxyds, flies off through the upper ſurface of the leaves, in company with heat and light, in the form of vital air." (Vide Mitchill on the decompoſition of contagious air by vegetation. New-York Mag. for 1797.)

The luxuriant growth of vegetables in the ſummer and autumn of 1795, in New-York, during the epidemic, makes it further evident, that vegetables decompound this noxious body, and thus act in a beneficial and ſalutary manner. Upon this principle in vegetables to deſtroy the chemical

G

union between the ingredients of feptous airs, may the dangerous confequences often attending the cutting down of woods in new and uncultivated countries, be accounted for. The exhalations from the fwamps, moraffes, &c. being fet loofe in greater quantity in the atmofphere, by the now more direct rays of the fun, without any adequate fupply of other vegetable fubftance to arreft and decompound them, they afcend, and pervade the air, carrying on their ufual noxious and deleterious qualities, on meeting the bodies of men, or brute creation.

6. The management of lazarettos may be conducted upon the fame principle. From the known mifcibility of contagion with water, and the fhort diftance thefe fluids extend their influence over this body, as has been repeatedly obferved by Lind, and others, the moft proper and healthy fituations for inftitutions of this kind, are readily pointed out. And,

7. According to what has been faid in the fifth chapter, concerning the production of contagious fluids in the ftomach and inteftinal tube, from animal and certain vegetable food, taken in from time to time, it will appear, that fuch fubftances as contain fepton to any amount, fuch as lean and mufcular animal fubftances, are improper ingredients in diet. Such articles, then, as contain none of this principle, ought to be felected as the moft proper for nourifhment in complaints occafioned by this acid. Fat or oily fubftances being of this clafs, and vegetables containing but little fepton, ought to be the moft beneficial and wholefome diet in ma-

lignant and peſtilential diſeaſes. This is authenticated by facts ſufficiently numerous to put it beyond cavil.

The comparative health, in the Weſt-Indies, between the Engliſh, who indulge in the free uſe of animal food, and the French, who, on the contrary, abſtain from this kind of aliment, and live principally on vegetable food, ſhews that animal matter is not only improper, but is an injurious article in our diet, in all peſtilential conditions of the atmoſphere, or when malignant diſeaſes prevail. The ſame is obſerved to happen in Bengal, and other parts of the Eaſt-Indies. The Engliſh, who live principally on animal and vegetable food, are far more liable to attacks of malignant diſeaſes, and a greater number of them are carried off annually thereby, than of the Gentoos and Brahmans, who live on rice. Beſide, it is well known how much leſs fatal the *yellow fever*, and other ſpecies of malignant diſeaſes, are among the negroes of the Weſt-Indies, and thoſe of the ſouthern ſtates, who live on vegetable food for the moſt part, than among the whites of theſe places, who are under no neceſſity of abſtaining from the uſe of animal food.

# APPENDIX.

## EXPERIMENT I.

I TOOK two mice; one I caufed to be ftung by a wafp, which was immediately thrown into con-vulfions, and expired in two minutes: into an incifion made in the mufcular fubftance of the other, I injected two drops of the nitrous acid; it feemed to operate exactly in the fame manner as the fting of the wafp, and the animal expired im-mediately. On opening them, and endeavouring to ftimulate the mufcular fubftance of their hearts, I found it had in a great meafure loft its irritability. Fontana obferves, in his book upon Poifons, that the nitrous acid, applied to the mufcular fubftance of a pigeon, killed it immediately; Cavendifh and Lavoifier have proved, by experiments, that the azote is the radical principle of the nitrous acid.

## EXPERIMENT III.

I took four young puppies: into the jugular vein of one, I injected four drops of the decoction of white helebore; into the fecond, I injected four drops of the digitalis; into the third, I injected one grain of the falt of urine diffolved in water; the fourth I caufed to be ftung by two wafps; the firft died almoft inftantaneoufly; the fecond and third in lefs than five minutes; the fourth recovered with great difficulty, and feemed to throw off the difeafe by foaming at the mouth.

## EXPERIMENT IV.

I caufed a number of earth worms to be ftung by bees, ants, and other infects, which always killed them immediately; and feemed to act on them in the fame manner as the decoction of the poifonous plants, the laurel, tobacco, opium, &c. This effect is aftonifhing, in thefe animals, which, when cut into pieces with the knife, ftill retain their irritability for many hours, or even days.

All poifonous plants with which we are acquainted feem to act in the fame manner when injected into the circulating fyftem of animals; yet, from the nature and conftruction of the ftomach of fome animals, they are eaten with impunity: goats will grow fat upon euphorbium, and fwine upon henbane, &c.

## THE END.